Gavilan Peak

The Struggle for Existence

Anatiposi

Gavilan Peak

The Struggle for Existence

Reprint of the original, first published in 1872.

1st Edition 2023 | ISBN: 978-3-38218-476-6

Anatiposi Verlag is an imprint of Outlook Verlagsgesellschaft mbH.

Verlag (Publisher): Outlook Verlag GmbH, Zeilweg 44, 60439 Frankfurt, Deutschland
Vertretungsberechtigt (Authorized to represent): E. Roepke, Zeilweg 44, 60439 Frankfurt, Deutschland
Druck (Print): Books on Demand GmbH, In de Tarpen 42, 22848 Norderstedt, Deutschland

THE

STRUGGLE FOR EXISTENCE.

BY

GAVILAN PEAK.

NEW YORK :

P. M. HAVERTY, PUBLISHER,

5 BARCLAY STREET.

1872,

JOSEPH J. LITTLE,
Stereotyper, Electrotyper, and Printer,
108 to 114 Wooster St., N. Y.

THE STRUGGLE FOR EXIST-ENCE.

ERE Progress turned things inside out,
And of old whimseys made a rout,
Our sins, it was believed by all,
Were wholly due to Adam's fall
　　And Beelzebub's existence.

But the disasters of our race
To Adam we no longer trace.
At last the devil has his due,
And Progress shows our faults ensue
　　From struggling for existence.

The houseless wretch by hunger led
To steal a shilling's worth of bread,
From honest circles we expel,
And punish with a convict's cell
　　His struggle for existence.

The place-man who betrays his trust,
And gains a heap of shining dust,
We find by far too great a man
To punish with our social ban
　　His struggle for existence.

But if there be no inbred rogue,
New morals will come into vogue,
And laws be made to suit the mode
By Progress, who will base her code
　　On the struggle for existence.

For sin being caused by what's without,
What judgment can be meted out
To sinners into sin betrayed
Only for lack of rightful aid
　　In the struggle for existence?

Oh, there will be some jolly laws!
And ev'ry judge who tries a cause
Will to the convict make rebate
Of what was due him from the State
　　In his struggle for existence.

Not only laws but all our views
Of right and wrong we will transfuse;
And for the baseness of the mind
An ample mantle we shall find
    In the struggle for existence.

Then Scaurus Bombyx, rich and old,
Will falsely swear to get more gold,
And think, "How sad my friends to peel,
Yet 'tis not av'rice makes me steal,
    But the struggle for existence."

Florus will tempt his Claudio's wife,
And say, "I have a right to life.
What's life without his Julia's charms?
And absent from his Julia's arms,
    I feel I've no existence."

Ventosus, swelling for a name,
Through dirty paths will tread to fame,
And sigh, "Foul paths through which I go!
And sometimes I stoop cursèd low
    In my struggle for existence."

Globus will suffer with the gout,
Nor own his sins have found him out.
You'll say, "High living sowed the seed."—
"*Why, dang it, sir, I had to feed*
In my struggle for existence."

When Bibulus is on the rack,
And feels his head about to crack,
You'll say, " 'Tis rum." *Good sir, just think*
That all of us are forced to drink
In our struggle for existence.

When Sporos, broke by heavy bets,
Weeps as his sun of frolic sets,
Our envy gone, perhaps we'll sigh,
"Alas! poor chap, he played too high
In his struggle for existence."

But Scaurus with more lib'ral ways,
Ventosus with less dirty bays,
Bibulus shunning brandy's charms,
And Florus in his own wife's arms,
Might still support existence.

And so might Globus with less *feed*,
And Sporos spending with less speed.
Say so to either, the answer—"Fudge!
You're not like me. How can you judge
    Of what to me's existence?"

Ay, that's the tender spot to touch!
Our needs so small, our wants so much;
And Progress may forever reign,
Yet fail to fix and render plain
    What constitutes existence.

THE NEW RELIGION.

Nor long ago there was a God,
Who governed all things by His nod
   Until upset by Progress.

'Tis found this God was but a notion,
Which now has ceded place to Motion,
   Another name for Progress.

All fealty to moral laws
And homage paid to ancient saws
   Are now transferred to Progress.

And but two sins are known below,
To stand stock-still, or move too slow
   To suit the taste of Progress.

Derisively to snarl and scold
At ev'rything that's six months old
   Is sanctified to Progress.

To ride a thousand miles a day,
And mind no object by the way,
   Is pilgrimage for Progress.

To have your body made a hash,
And served up at a railroad smash,
   Is martyrdom to Progress.

To have more land than we can till,
Though not more than our children will,
   Gives great offence to Progress.

To see a thinly-peopled state,
With taxes small and wages great,
    Gives great distaste to Progress.

To see a nation fine and grand,
A crowded, though a pauper land,
    Gives great delight to Progress.

For Progress says, "Run up the hill,
And then keep running on until
    You're at the foot through Progress."

But slowly up the hill to stray,
And loiter often by the way,
    Calls down the curse of Progress.

One's head with paper scrap to fill,
As 'twere a mash-tub in a mill,
    Is piety to Progress.

In language suited to a prude
To warm the fancy of the lewd,
    Is the decency of Progress.

To sting a heart through polished speech,
Then mildly against anger preach,
    The meekness is of Progress.

If anything by skill you frame,
You may alter, but not use the same,
    While in the Church of Progress.

To use a thing till quite outworn,
Is that which most provokes the scorn
    And petulance of Progress.

To do, undo, to mar, to mend,
To turn and change without an end,
    Are sacred rites to Progress.

A changeful masquerade is life,
With changeless passions ever rife,
　　Or fast or slow our progress,

And ye who seek to guide us, know
Our passions make the routes we go,
　　E'en in the Age of Progress.

TO THE LADIES

WHO WOULD SUBSTITUTE "THE TWO SEXES OF
MAN," FOR THE TERMS MEN AND WOMEN.

IT has always been held as a matter of course,
That a horse is no mare, though a mare is a horse.
Now, if this is good logic, deny it who can,
A man is no woman, but a woman's a man.
And now a wise woman whom the term woman vexes
Will have no more women, only men of two sexes
And pronounces it stupid, uncouth, and unfair
To not grant a woman what's allowed to a mare.
But the logic must change in respect to these classes,
If, for sexes of horses we put sexes of asses;
For the people have held from the farthest time back
That a "jack" is no "jenny" and a "jenny" no "jack."

TO MY DOG.

If, poor Tray, to your vivacity
I could add a man's capacity,
So that you could, like your betters,
Learn to speak and learn your letters;
Rise from that to reading, writing,
Even up to speech inditing,
Far as metaphysics wander,
Or the works of science ponder,
In short, become a dog of mind,
And shine like one of human kind,
Say, could I do this, would I?—No;
And this the reason why:
I'd spoil a dog, and lose a friend,
For intellect does no way tend
To brighten friendship's glow;
And that cant of moral art
That science purifies the heart,
Is but a specious lie.

If, poor Tray, you were thus lifted,
And with human gifts were gifted,
'Twould, among much else, ensue
That you'd be no longer true:
Your simple style, so free from brag,
And your spontaneous caudal wag
You'd surely lose, though not instanter,
And become a moral canter:
You'd leave off rough-and-tumble fighting,
And take to caution and backbiting;
Into your master's acts would pry,
And all your master's faults would spy,
And, him you now believe perfection
You'd find wide open to objection;
Thus, in place of whining for him,
You would soon be whining o'er him;
Would snap him up on his theology,
And scorn to yield or make apology;
Or over some small disputation
Grow bitter through mere explanation;
Regret a friendship so ill-founded,
And wish it were but better grounded—

No more grateful for a dinner
When you got it from a sinner.
And getting on this way still faster,
You would at last desert your master.
Might, even, by ambition led—
Not from your heart, Tray, but your head—
To raise yourself by sordid paction,
Join to oppose him with some faction.

No, Tray, I would not use the power
To give thee this corrupting dower;
But while I had an ounce of prog
  I'd keep thee honest and a dog.

A HAPPY MAN.

Happy the man whose mind can run
    In well-adjusted grooves,
Who, having once his course begun,
    In one way ever moves.
Two kinds of men he only knows,
    The good kind and the bad—
The good his friends, the bad his foes,
    And all the latter mad.

He hates just as his party hates;
    Loves as his party loves;
For nothing ever hesitates
    When party draws or shoves.
But if he chance his grooves to quit,
    Terrific is the rack;
His mind, for other roads unfit,
    Is a horse-car off the track.

TO ELIZABETH TEA-CADDY.

Fair counsel of the fairer sex,
Pray never more your temper vex
    By blowing up the males.
Your native and sophistic arts
Are needed for your sisters' hearts,
    To touch them with your tales.

You say their woe your bosom wrings;
But only mark the giddy things,
    They're looking at the beaux!
You tell them of the sorry plight
They're in for lack of suffrage right.
    They eye each other's clothes.

'Twas shrewd, the way you did begin,
For if you could but raise a din,
    You'd surely sweep the field.

Alone to make the clamor cease,
If not for justice, yet for peace,
  The men would surely yield.

But how your sisters' hearts to fire?
O! how to plant a new desire
  And make them long to vote?
O! how to swell the ballot-tide,
On which to place of trust and pride
  You fondly hope to float?

In one way can the feat be done,
Perchance with mischief, but with fun:
  Show them that by your plan,
Although they might have little weight
In all the high concerns of State,
  They each would have a man.

EPITHALAMIUM.

A L'AVENUE CINQUIÈME.

Blessings on the prudent bride
Now to Mister Nugget tied.
Naught cares she for flames and darts,
Nor for Cupid pinning hearts.
     The bridegroom's kind
     Because he's blind.
May both the joys they look for find.

Mister Nugget's well-to-do:
Coach has he and horses too.
O, it is a splendid match!
Bride has made a lucky catch;
     For wedded joys
     Bring girls and boys,
But not the tin to buy the toys.

Cupid fans the bridegroom's fire:
Plutus moves the bride's desire:
Hymen sanctifies the bond
'Tween the prudent and the fond,
    For Plutus' aid
    Half Hymen's trade
Has furnished since the world was made.

LINES

TO YOUR GREATEST FAVORITE, DEAR READER.

CHIEF privy-counsellor of beaux and belles,
Trim modish gentlemen and flashy swells,
Maids old or young, rakehellies when beginning
Anew their courses of promiscuous sinning,
Of pompous doctor and of pulpit prig,
Of fat official proud of belly big,
Of poets who affect a languid air,
Of all who love to go *en militaire*,
Of dandies of all ages, sorts, and sizes,
And of the sage who says he thee despises,
Your one great priv'lege is in all you greet
To have the sunny side alone to meet.
The guarded look, the dollar-born disdain,
The girlish pout, the twinge of secret pain,

Ill-humor, dullness, and censorious pride
Are in thy cheering presence cast aside,
And, howe'er old and stern may be the fellow,
His look to self-complacency thou'lt mellow.
Nor is't by flatt'ry that you win the heart:
The HONEST DEALER is thy only part.
But truth from thee has never yet offended,
And all who meet thee think themselves com-
    mended.

O thou infallible, yet honest, minion!
Thou censor that hast all men's good opinion,
My state I'd change for thine, could I but pass
From what I am and be a looking-glass.

ADAH'S ADDRESS TO DEATH.

Shall I no more in poets' arms
    Poetic raptures weave?
The thronging men who prize my charms
    Shall I no more receive?
Must I exchange for thee, O Death,
    Their stampings and hurrahs?
Pleasure I must give up with breath,
    But I'll not give up applause.

I will in verse, or prose that's had
    The fever called broke-bone,
For my mad pranks in strains as mad,
    By penitence atone:
And to the very latest time
    A wonder it will be
How one of sentiment sublime,
    Could live from shame so free.

From childhood's hour I've felt a rage
   To make the public stare.
I've ridden *bareback* on the stage,
   Myself almost as bare.
My breath I'll quit, but not my art:
   I'll close with Death, and then
Draw a whole season in the part
   Of Mary Magdalen.

COUNT STOLZEN.

Count Stolzen he lived on a bank of the Rhine,
    But never upon his own rhino,
And though he was fond of the juice of the vine,
    He never did drink his own wine O.

He built not his castle, nor bought it with gold,
    But took it from old Baron Wouter.
The Baron was weak, and the Count he made bold
    To take it because he was stouter.

This castle was built on the top of a rock,
    Though in it was never a rocker:
On every door the bold Count had a lock,
    But not his own shot in the locker.

Count Rhenze lived near with his daughter so fair—
   His heir, and so Stolzen besought her;
But Stolzen was told he could not have this heir,
   So in ambush he lay for and caught her.

But never a guilder made Stolzen thereby;
   The dad was a cunning contriver.
He said, "I will get me a son, if I die,
   And Stolzen shall not have a stiver."

A maiden he married ere one week had run,
   And well the old fellow maintained her;
In less than a year he had got him a son,
   By means of a favored retainer.

And Ulric this favored retainer was hight.
   A short man he was and a burly;
A good-natured man at a feast or a fight;
   At other times, though, he was surly.

When Stolzen was told that there was heir male
   To what he so fiercely was after,
So wildly he swore, that his pages turned pale
   When caught giving way to their laughter.

But Rhenze soon found what some others may find
   In getting an heir by a proxy,
And, though to her fun so 'conveniently blind,
   He got a fell dose from his doxy.

No coaxing the widow's wild sorrow could tame,
   Nor would she the least cease her fury
Till Ulric, her husband *de facto*, became
   Not *de facto* alone, but *de jure*.

Now Ulric was master of Rhenze's broad land,
   The Count seized the daughter to hang her,
But finding no suitable rope near at hand,
   He set him at work first to bang her.

A crack he had given her ere she cried out,
   "Why, husband dear, wherefore this clatter?
Go mad, if you will, but think what it's about.—
   Sit down, and let's argue this matter."

Count Stolzen, of reasoning men though a type,
   Yet added a finishing whack, O;
Then ordered some ale, but he ordered no pipe
   Because he could get no tobacco.

The war being over, they sat down as friends,
　　More loving for this little bicker;
They argued what projects would best serve their
　　ends,
　　And duly disposed of their liquor.

"By G—d!" cried the Count, "were it not for the
　　ban—"
　　And bang came his fist on the table—
"I'd seize on the castle and kill ev'ry man."
　　His Countess said, "If you were able.

"Now policy, husband, is best for the trade
　　That we at this time should be driving;
You manage her brute and to me leave his jade,
　　And soon our affair will be thriving.

"For Ulric can lead more than twenty-five men
　　To every five you can jog to,
And has what you're sure of not three days in ten,
　　An ample supply of good prog too."

The Count called a page, and said, "Summon
    the priest;
I want him to write me a letter."
"My lord, Father Rudolph's as drunk as a beast;
    The Abbot can do the work better."

"Why, then, to the Abbey, boy, hie thee—away!
    Take Henwig and Ludwig along, sir;
If Abbot and inkhorn you bring not to-day,
    Your life you may sell for a song, sir."

The Abbot they found at his twentieth course:
    They lifted him into a saddle,
And forced him to measure the breadth of a horse,
    Though he vowed he was too fat to straddle.

Arrived at the castle, the Count and his train
    Were horsed and just ready to sally.
"Sir Priest," said the Count, as he drew in his
    rein,
    "For blessing alone can I dally.

" But wait my return and give way to no fears;
   We'll have, I can tell you, a jolly day:
Hard by there's a town I've protected for years,
   As you'd fat a hen for a holiday."

He rode through this town did the Count with
    an air
   That made the good burghers feel easy,
Till he'd got closely penned in the market-place
    square,
   The Aldermen stupid and greasy.

And when all was ready he gave 'em a look,
   Which only a lordling can muster,
And lowered so long that the Aldermen shook,
   And seemed in a terrible fluster.

" Ye cowardly, miserly, false-hearted knaves!"
   At last he burst forth like the thunder,
" Is't thus ye would pay for protection, ye slaves?"
   This made all the Aldermen wonder.

"My man you have murdered—my stout Iden-
    stein."
  The Aldermen now stood confounded.
"But look ye, I swear ye shall hang ere I dine,
    Unless the foul deed be compounded."

And Stolzen would not from their borders depart,
  Nor call their account as all squared off,
Till horses and men and a heavy ox-cart
  Had all they could possibly bear off.

But as to the murder he laid to their charge,
  The Count did amazingly fib it;
For, caught by the Emperor's men when at large,
  The knave had been swung on a gibbet.

Fine jest for the Count, and, returned with his
    ware,
  His Countess did fondly caress him.
The Abbot, who thought he was in for a share,
  Did also most fervently bless him.

Full one quarter part of this well-gotten spoil
   For Ulric the pair had intended,
For that, as a sauce for the family broil,
   The Countess had strongly commended.

But justly to lay this full quarter part out
   Most strangely and sorely perplexed 'em.
They found not a thing they could well do without:
   To part with a penny's worth vexed 'em.

To send all the wine was the Countess inclined,
   If only to help end the puzzling;
This only disgusted the other one's mind,
   Addicted as he was to guzzling.

"These gewgaws," cried Stolzen, "now I will be
     bound,
   Will do up the business quite nicely!"
The Countess now tried 'em, and very soon found
   They suited her humor precisely.

2*

The Count to abandon his liquor was loath,
  The lady would not lose her frippery;
And thus it remained for a week with 'em both,
  So much were they given to grippery.

The letter, however, was written the while,
  But the Abbot, good man, did not write it;
He took all its credit for polish of style,
  But ordered a priest to indite it.

The Abbot, although a most reverend man,
  To learning was not the least partial:
But potent he was with the full flowing can,
  And early in life had been martial.

Their pleasant disputing, of course, at last brought
  The Count and the Countess to high words.
His speech with most horrible cursing was fraught,
  And hers was well sprinkled with bywords.

At length from his drink the old Abbot rushed in,
  Aroused by their cursing and bawling,

And showed by his manner of stopping their din
  His wit and the worth of his calling.

He made 'em both swear on a true martyr's bone
  An oath of the greatest precision—
To leave the partition to his will alone
  And strictly abide his decision.

He said to the Count, "You must keep all your
    wine,
  I'll stay with you here to help drink it."
He said to the Countess, "'Tis meet you go fine,
  And you must keep every trinket.

"The rest of the booty is heaped up in bulk
  I'll halve it by truest of measure,
But first I will take all the plate from the hulk
  As the Virgin's just share of the treasure."

The men with these gifts were then ordered to ride
  To Ulric's and there to expose 'em.
The eyes of his people they opened so wide,
  For days they had trouble to close 'em.

This treasure did Ulric's mind rapidly free
  From errors with which it was tainted.
Count Stolzen no longer he reckoned to be
  So black as he always was painted.

His crimes he had deemed of the murkiest shade,
  And hellish his commonest dealings:
Those crimes turned to errors when thus he was made
  A sharer in one of his stealings.

These presents, indeed, proved a true golden chain
  To neighborly bind these two houses:
The chiefs soon became a most brotherly twain;
  As loving as sisters, their spouses.

Count Stolzen could count in his well-chosen band
  For every crime a fine jobber,
At poisoning more than one capital hand,
  And many a dexterous robber.

Now Ulric to these dirty business could shift,
  While living as strict as a parson,
And, keeping his dignity, share in the thrift
  Of sacrilege, murder, and arson.

The Countess when winning the Count to her view
　　Had said, "Why I wish you to tarry
Is this: we've a girl, they a boy, and the two
　　May some day be wishing to marry."

Through fate and finessing all truly fell out
　　In accord with the lady's prediction.
The Pope, too, who knew of the proxy, no doubt,
　　Said nothing about interdiction.

RAIN AND UMBRELLAS.

THE sun sets dimly with his phiz as red
As an old toper's when he goes to bed,
Though, may be, he's but angry with the cloud
That his declining majesty would shroud.
Yet one who's weather-wise beholds him set,
And says the signs are sure for heavy wet.
The wind has blown due easterly all day,
And eastern winds bring rain, the wise ones say.

Well, as the roads are dusty, let it rain
And wash in Betty's place my window-pane.
It may make promenaders cry, " Alas! "
But farmers all will say, " 'Tis good for *sass*,"
And even hail a three days' dripping fog
To turn the ground into a squashy bog.
So, speed the plough, and let the rain come down :
Without the country what would be the town ?
But 'lackaday ! it saddens me to think
That when our thirsty Mother takes a drink
Without the usual notice being sent,
Dingy and damp, that such is her intent,
The imbibition urges man to crime
Which 'scapes the law, but shall not 'scape my rhyme.
When sudden drops begin the streets to spatter,
The nimble cits straightway begin to scatter—
All but the few old denizens so queer
Who seem to think it April all the year :
They roofs of cotton o'er their heads display,
And undisturbed pursue their plodding way.
From under awnings many watch the damp,
Irresolute to take the sloppy tramp.

From cellar door-ways others view with ease
The lifted skirts expose the snowy knees.
But all who can, rush to a neighboring friend,
In hopes he has an *umberel* to lend.
Thus Jenkins from reluctant Jones will borrow
His sole umbrella, "only till the morrow."
The morrow comes; Jenkins has 'scaped a soak,
But looks upon his promise as a joke.
Fine joke for him! No joke at all to Jones,
Who all unomnibused, wet to the bones,
Politeness with the rheumatiz' atones.
Such scurvy tricks may all who do them rue.
If friend of mine had not umbrellas two,
Not far apart, but in one place together,
I'd scorn to borrow and would brave the weather.
But could my friend to me an umbrella spare,
I'd guard it with the most religious care,
And when the clouds had ceased their aqueous pranks
Would send it back to him with many thanks.
Be they of silk or cotton, black or blue,
This moral of umbrellas will hold true:
However oft you lose your own umbrellas,
You have no right to smouch another fellow's.

MONKEYS ON HORSEBACK.

THESE days of ours indeed are doubting days.
Lord Bacon now 'tis claimed wrote Shakespeare's plays:
As if all Bacon wrote and Shakespeare too
Were but a trifle for one mind to do—
As if the lore of passion came unsought,
Or matchless lines for pastime could be wrought!
It is the itch of saying something strange
That leads the mind so far from reason's range;
And common minds despairing to excel,
Yet not content to be obscure and well,
Trust all to oddity, and contempt will dare,
Rather than not secure a general stare.
'Twas thus a certain postruer was led,
Though less by love of glory than for bread,
To walk where only bugs had walked before,
That is, upon the ceiling, not the floor.

AN ARGUMENT

AT THE ROSE AND THISTLE.

Two friends met at the "Rose and Thistle"
To smoke and chat and wet the whistle.
They talked at first about machinery,
But, branching off to rural themes,
They grew quite eloquent on scenery;
For both were cits who cherished dreams
That through their money-getting schemes
Ripe age would pay their chapman-strife
With quiet and a country life.

One was from England, and contended
That nature there and art were blended,
And hence that in Britannia's Isle
Beauty must wear her choicest smile.
"Of beauty nature's but a part,
And without nature what is art?
But take the two, sir, in connection,
And you have absolute perfection."

"Your maxim, sir, perhaps is sound,"
The other said, with hesitation,
"But truthful maxims may be found
Quite wrong in application.
Nature and art in graceful guise
In England show themselves together,
But, owing to obscuring skies,
Not often in the finest weather.
Still, not their union is the test,
But, *have they there both done their best?*
Sure, Italy has a brighter clime,
While Switzerland is more sublime;
Then, suited to one's lonely moods,
Far stretch the New World's solitudes:
And, not to touch too many topics,
There's the luxuriance of the tropics.
But this with deference I say,
Because, being in this country bred,
I cannot tell how far I may
By prejudice be led."

He made this liberal concession
To draw the other to confession

That the point on which they were divided
By neither could be well decided;
"But," cried the Briton, "Sir, no wonder
That you have made so great a blunder,
Since prejudice has made you blind.
Now, you must know, sir, that my mind
From prejudice is wholly free,
And therefore you can clearly see
That while your view must be mistaken,
Mine cannot be the least bit shaken,
And that your arguments must fall,
Since prejudice has sapped them all."

To arrogance one never can give way,
And hope by meekness to secure fair play;
For, if to placate some vain-glorious chap,
You pluck a single feather from your cap,
Unblushingly he'll put it in his own,
And as you lower yours will raise his tone.

ON A PLAY-BILL.

THAT huge high-colored placard is a lie—
The one announcing Miss Amanda Spry.
'Twas Puffer made her. He but dashed his pen,
Presto—Amanda was comedienne!
Miss Spry has legs, good bust, and rolling eye,
Manner familiar, spirits prompt and high;
Knows how to read, but scarcely how to spell;
Has sold her virtue, but has yet to sell.
In point of talent fit for third *soubrette*,
But Puffer lauds her, and she's first coquette.
Read his announcement that Thalia's come.
Puffer proclaims it. Let the town be dumb.

TWO INDEPENDENT VOTERS.

Smith.
NOTHING I more detest than party strife.

Brown.
It seems to me with ev'ry danger rife.

Smith.

Then, I presume that you pursue my plan,
To never scan his party, but the man.

Brown.

Exactly so.—But you'll admit, I know,
My party has———

Smith.

   Your party has! So, so!
I thought you'd given up party. But, proceed.

Brown.

Sir, I have principles.—Not for them I plead,
But for a man in ev'ry virtue decked.

Smith.

Your candidate, sir, has my full respect.

Brown.

Then, I am sure, sir, he will have your voice.

Smith.

Not quite so fast, sir; he is not my choice.

Brown.

Do you oppose him, sir, because he's good?

Smith.

I do.

Brown.

  Ho, ho!

Smith.

Let me be understood.
The better man he is the greater ill
With his false creed so high a place to fill.
An able man and good who yields to error
Is than a vicious fool a greater terror.
His very goodness leads him more astray,
And blinds him to the error of his way.
His virtues, too, his followers' faults sublime,
And his good life's a mantle for their crime.

Brown.

Good gracious! you're indeed a foe to party—
At least to one, and curse that one right hearty.

Smith.

No party, sir, has any weight with me.

Brown.

Oh, not the smallest!—But, sir, let me see.
My candidate you'd shun, though he were sainted.
Then, you'll not vote, for yours, you know, is
    tainted?

Smith.

He's not quite what he ought to be, 'tis true;
But he's *our* man, sir, and we'll make him do.

TO MOVE A PUPPET YOU MUST KNOW THE STRING.

"Jenkins," said Jones, "our mining scheme moves
    slow.—
With Podd, at any rate, it will not go.
He first talked *offish*, as if up to snuff,
And when I pressed it left me in a huff."
"But, Jones," said Jenkins, "I have got his name."
"Our Podd's?" cried Jones. "Yes," Jenkins said,
    "the same."
"What could you say that I did not, I wonder!"
"Nothing to him, Jones. I repaired your blunder.
You went direct to Podd. I went to Stout—
The only way, sir, to make Podd shell out.
Podd has no brains with all his loads of tin,
And always waits for Stout to say 'go in.'"
Thus o'er a gangway-plank a mule is led:
To start the mule a horse is put ahead.

WHITE LIES.

ONE must have boldness to temerity
To meet politeness with sincerity.

Such courage had a Mister Gruff,
A fellow of the coarsest stuff;
Who, though he felt a banker's pride,
Had in his boyhood porgies cried,
And oft, no doubt, to urge their sale
Had called them fresh when they were stale.

Gruff, after many invitations,
To a suburb village went to dine
With friends who, though in the market line,
Had genteel aspirations.
The hostess had bestowed her care
To cause her city guest to stare
Both at her food and dishing,
And to secure her meed of praise,
She used those common tortuous ways
Which are vanity's back-action—
That hinting sort of self-detraction

That's vulgarly called fishing.
" You must excuse us for our pease.
I fear, sir, they're too old to please."
Now, this was true, and so the boor
Said, "Madam, your peas are very poor."
The hostess felt this rude rebuff,
But still went on, though in a huff,
With her assumed humility;
And Gruff, who thought the dinner bad,
Drove his kind hostess almost mad
By his honest incivility.
At last was brought the housewife's pride.
The dame, recovering from her dumps,
Prepared to play her ace of trumps—
The pastry to divide.
" Our pastry is too poor to offer,
But I venture, sir, to make the proffer."
" Pie-crust," said Gruff, "I do detest.
I never eat the very best.
'Twill give dyspepsia, ma'am, to dogs,
And country pastry's fit for hogs."
" *Why, Mister Gruff, if that be true,*
It surely must be fit for you."

3

POMPONIUS BOMBYX.

In present fancy lives one's share of fame.
The madman, certain of a deathless name,
From that conception as much joy receives
As e'en the greatest hero e'er achieves.

Pomponius Bombyx viewed the rich parade
Of marble in a cemetery's shade,
And grew elated with the pleasing thought
That, as such sculptured honors can be bought,
He from his store might easily provide
To crown his dust with monumental pride.
Raised expectation made rich Bombyx glad,
But further thinking caused him to be sad.
"Of my fine monument what can I know
When I am quiet in the earth below?
But," he exclaimed, and pleasure lit his brow,
"I'll raise my monument and enjoy it now!"

THE TWO SEXES OF MAN.

For ev'ry doctrine there's a root
  In fact and reason,
However oddly it may shoot,
  And out of season.
A germ of truth o'er-nursed by passion
Will grow in most amazing fashion.

From germs of truth that doctrine grew
  So makes us wonder,
That man is man and woman too,
  Parted by blunder—
That, sex apart, there's no division
Which marks the sexes with precision.

'Tis Florus greets you. O his hand,
  How soft it presses!
Beneath his hat in wavy band
  Escape his tresses.
His skin is fair. His cheek is blooming.
His air both pliant and assuming.

Is it a woman in disguise?
  Not a whit tougher.
Its voice throws doubt on such surmise,
  Than woman's rougher.
But nature not the man expressing,
You'd doubt the fact, but for the dressing.

Florus, adieu! Here comes a dame
  With skin like leather,
Cov'ring a well-compacted frame
  Fit for all weather.
Round those thin lips no Cupids hover,
Nor would that brow invite a lover.

There's pith of business in her tone
  And in her diction,
And though her dress is woman's own,
  That may be fiction.
A stranger might with doubt be harried:
A friend cannot, for she is married.

Were all men of hard Alcon's mould
  Of brain and muscle,

And fitted both to fend and hold
    In life's stern tussle,
Or women all like Delia, pleasing,
These questions never would be teasing.

The types of woman and of man
    Must aye be granted.
We're never doubtful of the plan,
    Save when 'tis scanted.
But from the types extremes so vary,
There's seed for many a wild vagary.

CLIO SNUBBED.

WHAT precious loads of history fill our shelves!
    How little of it gets into our heads!
We are too busy with our precious selves
    To care for heroes in their narrow beds.

And what can all this pompous history teach
    That 'mongst ourselves we cannot better learn?

Say, priests of Clio, what is there you preach
   To which you have not given a party turn?

But were you free from warping of the mind,
   From partial records could you truth reveal?
What but mere dates and titles can you find
   Not marred or magnified by party zeal?

Can we call up the spirits of the dead
   And question them as we would living men?
Must not one form such spirits in his head,
   And out of matter furnished by the pen?

Form twenty models, if you please, and choose
   The one of Cæsar you may think the best,
Still you your judgment or your fancy use:
   There is no stamp which can its truth attest.

You'll weigh its truth by standards you have seen,
   Some friends, it may be, of imperious will.
By present men we judge what men have been;
   From our own scene some fancied scene we fill.

Augustus Cæsar! what made him august?
   Such prudent men we see on ev'ry hand.

Not his bright genius, but his weighty trust;
　Not merit, but position made him grand.

As bold, ingenious robbers go unsung,
　As ever blazoned an historic page.
Commerce no less can boast the wheedling tongue,
　Than can diplomacy on its grander stage.

Who grasps at empire makes the nations gaze;
　But a projector in the busy mart,
Concerning whom we ask but how he pays,
　May act as dexterous and as bold a part.

All that makes history all around us lives
　The common qualities from which actions spring.
The action's stamp the aspiration gives,
　Whether it move a peasant or a king.

Yet from recorded life one truth we know,
　Its mazy lines no matter how we scan,
For all the pages of its volumes show
　How changeless yet how full of change is man.

For man, so varied from his first rude birth,
　Keeps the one course his passions make him run.
So ever flies the ever-changing earth
　In its accustomed path around the sun.

WHO ARE HAPPY?

Who are happy? Not the wise:
They suspect the cup of pleasure.
Not happy he whose cautious eyes
Let slip the joys that they would measure.
  Happiness is not in riches;
  They bring anxious cares.
 As to women, drat the witches!
   They are naught but snares.
    With food replete
    We cannot eat:
   What hunger gave is lost.
    To wine we flee,
    But ev'ry spree
   A headache's sure to cost.
    At cards we're tricked:
    At dice we're nicked:
For ev'ry sport there's penance fixed.

Should care not with our pleasure blend,
  Nor hushed anxiety,

Soon would our unmixed pleasure end
  In flat satiety.
Not in ease, nor yet in action,
   But in all earth's round
Happiness is only found
   In self-satisfaction.
Then hail, chief friend of our poor race,
   All hail, Assurance!
Sustainer of the human breast,
Thou giv'st to life unfailing zest:
   Sans thee 'tis mere endurance.
Smart child of Impudence and Vanity,
   Protean as humanity,
    All hail! as now with painted face,
    In silks and velvets, gems and lace,
    You proudly strut—
    A brazen slut,
Resplendent in the wage of shameless lust,
Looking on honest rags as clothing meaner dust.

Be twenty little things all in a minute.
A little miss, her dress her only care,
With mincing step and perky, smirky air,
   3*

And little tossed-up head with nothing in it.
Or be a flutt'ring fop;
Twitter before this miss, then to that one hop,
Be poetaster, smallest of small things,
That weekly weakly sings;
Or little amateur of fiddle,
Who squeaking,
Creaking,
A *Berlioz* ready made,
Leaves useful trade
To bore his neighbor's ears and friends to diddle.

But you've need for all your art,
If you'll play your leading part,
And to us now the full fledged beau,
The happiest of mortals show.
Happy in his figure,
Be it short or tall,
Slender, crooked, or meagre
Or round as any ball.
Happy in his figure; happier in his clothes:
Ev'ry day repeating the mutations of the rose.
Budding in the morning
When arising from his bed;

Half-blown his adorning
With the frizzing of his head.
Then comes the glory of the padded vest;
Bijouterie next, brilliant, if not the best;
Then torturing boots, less elegant than tight;
Then speckless coat; then gloves of color light;
A small cane dandled—lustrous hat for crest—
In hour of perfect bloom he issues forth full drest,
And seems to tread on air, such rapture fills his breast.

See the man of ability
Cursed with humility!
How he shrinks
As he thinks
He sees more than his peers in those round him.
He sees through presumption,
Yet bows to assumption,
And not lacking learning,
Nor yet discerning,
Any ass may at pleasure confound him.
He retreats from disdain,
Yet he nurses his pain—
Pain ever corroding.

The appalling word fail
Makes his heart ever quail
And disaster is ever forboding,
Till lonely he slinks to a corner
The riddle and laugh of the scorner;
Sees effrontery grasp of merit the prize,
Tames his heart to his fate and despondingly dies.

O vanity! thou painting sun
That givest life its hues
And makest it a revel,
O teach me self-distrust to shun,
That pest'lent breeder of the blues
And conjuror of the devil.
Teach me myself to raise
To the summit of self-praise:
Inward let me turn my ear
And delighted let me hear
In the resonance of vaunting,
In the echo of self-chaunting,
The world my merit landing:
O, happy let me be, like those who do their own
applauding.

ONE'S HEAD SHOULD GROW OLD WITH ONE'S SHOULDERS.

SAYS Codrus, who, in discipline precise,
To all is ever lavish with advice:
"It is the turn for taking things apart
Has given our modern era such a start.
Would we be wiser than the ancient Greek,
But that in atoms we for atoms seek?
The viewless mite submitted to dissection
Reveals wee parts for more minute inspection;
For 'tis by almost shutting Nature out
We gain a clue to what she is about.
So, sir, if you would rightly school your boy,
Teach him to analyze as his first employ."

"Codrus, not so. I think 'twere just as fit
Ere reason blooms to force the buds of wit.
Though wit the mind may more than reason please,
We grow to wit by far more slow degrees.

And more important 'tis to know the way
To use our reason than with reason play.
Not that I mean analysis should sit
Apart from order by the side of wit,
But that of reason 'tis no matin flower,
And blooms much nearer to its noontide hour.
The knowledge that is patent to the eye
Is that to which the mind should first apply,
The while by action we ourselves reveal,
And learn to know the mind by what we feel;
For of philosophy the proper ground
Is what we feel within and see around;
And if this basis be not understood,
Minute inspection will do little good.
The child should teach us ere we teach the child.
Who breaks the colt and lets the horse run wild?
Life is not long enough to compass art:
Why seek to cram it into youth's small part?
Yet the proud father fondly thinks his son
Should be turned out complete at twenty-one.

"Survey the ground since first the arts began
And follow Nature's course in teaching man.

With what the sky above and earth below
Could to his prompt, unaided vision show,
He grew familiar first, nor less he sought
To mark the bearings and the course of thought
Ere Nature let him chemic tests apply,
Or search remoter wonders in the sky.
Still must the world be new to ev'ry boy--
Its objects wonders and its actions joy.
Then follow Nature: to invert her plan
Might spoil a boy, and would not make a man."

COARSE WARES HAVE THE WIDER MARKET.

THE earlier Wits, who Nature sought
    As guide and inspiration,
By her to please the sense were taught
    In art's elaboration;
But Nature now the Wits deny.
    The latest dispensation
Is, "Do your best to crucify
    The sense by mere sensation."

ENVY WEARS A THOUSAND MASKS.

BALBUS, whose wit is great but learning small,
Cries out on scholars as mere plodders all;
Jeers a quotation as a vain parade,
And mocks when mention of a book is made.
Doubtless his judgment makes him thus condemn,
And not mere envy of more learnèd men;
But wherefore does he make so much ado,
When by some chance he reads a page or two?

TO AUTHORS.

THE untried author, when he takes the field,
Uses his preface only as his shield;
But praise will make him use it for his pride,
And burnish that which he should cast aside.
Its polished face he'll hold in such a way
As makes a mirror for his own display.
Such looking-glass reflections, dear to all,
Are for the public, not the private hall:
For one's own vanity is lawful king;
Another's but a paltry, upstart thing.
He who will sound his own praise in his book,
Will go a-fishing with a naked hook.
And if he bait his hook with modest phrase,
'Twill not avail to catch him any praise;
For by such art he'll show that his intent
Is not to snatch, that he may circumvent.

Praise is a dish set on a public shelf,
Yet he is d——d who carves it for himself,
However hungry. In an author's case
One's not allowed to show a wishing face.
In this regard an author's like a dog
That in the market dares not smell the prog
Without the butcher-boys begin to rail,
Or his good master pays him with a blow.
Yet all expect the dog to wag his tail,
No matter whether he be fed or no.

———————

PROSPERO.

————

"I joy," said Prospero, "that I inherit
Not riches only, but a stoic spirit.
Why is it, prithee, we so seldom find
Serenity dependent on the mind?
Why, in this letter which I just have read
A bankrupt merchant fears he'll want for bread.

Fears he'll want bread when labor's in demand
To lay down railroads and to till the land!
Fears he'll want bread while he has limbs for hire!
'Twould serve him right to let the wretch expire."
As Prospero capped the climax of disdain
A letter came that stopped his moral strain.
'Twas sealed with black. It trembled in his hand,
And his face altered as its lines he scanned.
"*What is the matter?*" I inquired with dread;
"My uncle, sir," he faltered out, "is dead."
"*'Twas much you loved him, his death shakes you so;*
But time, my Prospero, will assuage the blow."
"No, though I fawned on him till I was sick,
I loathed the rascal as I do Old Nick.
His dying, sir, I'd not have taken ill,
If the old ass had named me in his will."

"Ye cowardly, miserly, false-hearted knaves!"
   At last he burst forth like the thunder,
"Is't thus ye would pay for protection, ye slaves?"
   This made all the Aldermen wonder.

MELISSA SHARP.

New love and true is all composed of praise.
This flattery knows and counterfeits its ways.
When love grows cold praise may revive its flame,
As may a spark the fire from which it came.
Praise, love's first-born, let love not throw away;
The child may nurse its mother in decay.
Nor let a flatt'rer lay aside her lure
And think her bird when caught forever sure.

Melissa Sharp her marriage bargain made—
By all esteemed a handsome stroke of trade—
To soothe her pride laid by her wheedling plan
And treated with reserve her captured man.
She loved his purse, but scorned his empty head,
And thought she paid him when she shared his bed.
He knew her witty and believed her true,
But felt himself defrauded of his due.

Estranged from home, he now a mistress keeps,
While scorned Melissa hugs her pride and weeps.
"Better," she cries, "far better to be dead,
Than spurned for one I know is underbred!
O what a fool to love such looks—such ways!"

"Not her he loves, Melissa, but her praise.
She'll praise his gloves, his handkerchief, his hat;
For such light flattery will please a flat.
But 'tis the central feature of his face
By which she hopes to lengthen your disgrace.
With admiration of its shape she glows,
And thus she leads your husband by the nose."

THE MACHINE IN ART.

GOOD Dame Progress, you're too fussy!
  Right or wrong, you can't be still;
Free-eyed Art you've now infected
  With the spirit o' the mill.

Pawing Pegasus, no longer
  A skyward soaring horse,
Trots in harness now for purses,
  'Gainst time around a course.

We have but to leave our orders
  In regard to price and style,
To have "history," or landscape
  By the yard, or by the mile.
And what vastness of production
  In the line of prints is seen!
Due alone to imitation
  And the aid of the machine.

How uniform the excellence
  Both prints and canvas show!
All aiming to be regular
  And neither high nor low.
In the medial ideal
  No coarseness can have place
The drapery is point device
  And classical each face.

Art's ideal now is elegance,
  As in furnishing a hall,
Where we can achieve but splendor,
  And fashion's all in all.
But customary elegance
  Is commonplace at best:
The plain are never beautiful,
  However richly drest.

Free as Guido's famed Aurora,
  Art in learning's dawn arose,
But now she's prim Miss Nancy,
  And minces on her toes.
Far better than such niceness,
  Where impulse never glows,
Is the least of Rembrandt's etchings,
  Or a whim of *Jacques Callot's.*

TO THE READER.

READER, with our kind adieu
Take this recipe with you:

If you find your temper gay,
Then care only for to-day.
If beside you should sit Sorrow,
Then think only of to-morrow.
Present joys will thus be tasted,
And Hope's illusions not be wasted.
And may Time thus ever find you
With Joy to cheer, or Hope to blind you.